This Little Tiger book belongs to:

_____

_____

_____

This book is dedicated to Claudia and Kate
(and long-suffering mums everywhere) ~ LP

LITTLE TIGER PRESS LTD,
an imprint of the Little Tiger Group
1 Coda Studios, 189 Munster Road, London SW6 6AW
Imported into the EEA by Penguin Random House Ireland,
Morrison Chambers, 32 Nassau Street, Dublin D02 YH68
www.littletiger.co.uk

First published in Great Britain 2008
This edition published 2018

Text and illustrations copyright © Liz Pichon 2008
Liz Pichon has asserted her right to be identified
as the author and illustrator of this work under the
Copyright, Designs and Patents Act, 1988

ISBN 978-1-78881-034-0
Printed in China
LTP/1800/3818/0521
10 9 8 7 6 5 4 3 2

The Three Horrid Pigs

and the
Big Friendly Wolf

Liz Pichon

LITTLE TIGER
LONDON

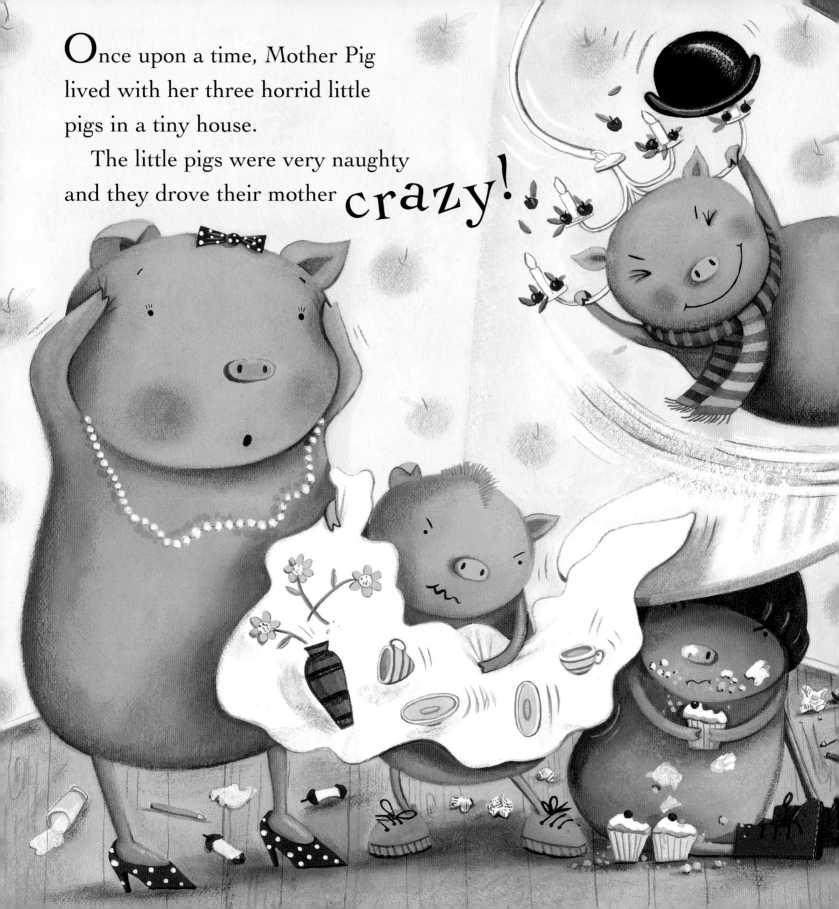

Once upon a time, Mother Pig lived with her three horrid little pigs in a tiny house.

The little pigs were very naughty and they drove their mother crazy!

"I've had enough of you pesky pigs," she told them. "It's about time you moved out and found your own way in the world!"

So she packed their bags and *sent them on their way.*

Go on, clear off!

Stop pushing!

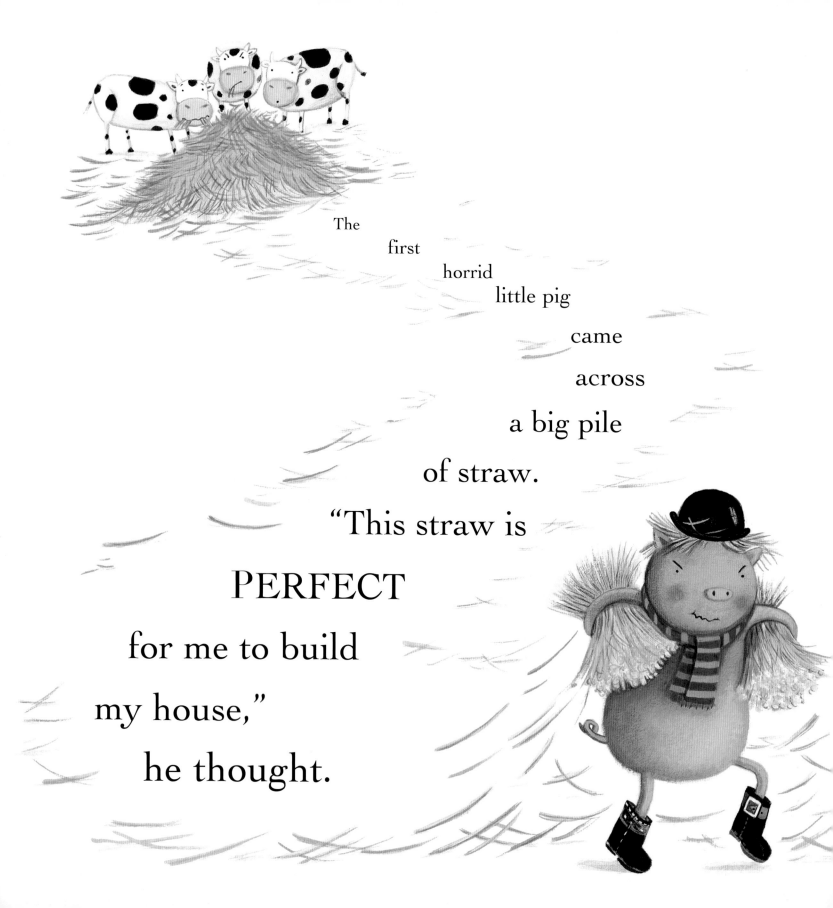

The
first
horrid
little pig
came
across
a big pile
of straw.
"This straw is
PERFECT
for me to build
my house,"
he thought.

But the little pig was lazy. And he didn't make his straw house very strong at all.
Luckily, a big friendly wolf (who just happened to be a builder) was passing by.
"Good grief!" gasped the wolf. "What a mess that house is. I'll go and see if I can help."

Gasp!

That'll do!

"Little pig, little pig, may I come in?" asked the wolf. **"PUSH OFF!"** shouted the pig. "Not by the hairs on my chinny chin chin will I let a **WOLF** in!

Put one paw on my house

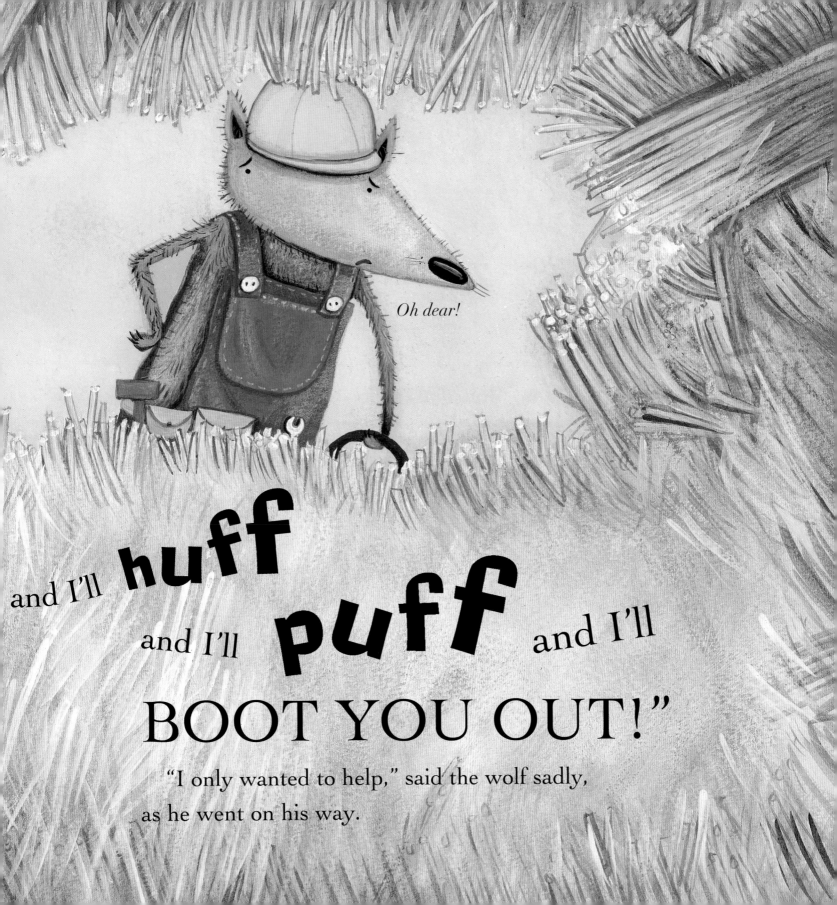

Oh dear!

and I'll **huff** and I'll **puff** and I'll BOOT YOU OUT!"

"I only wanted to help," said the wolf sadly,
as he went on his way.

The second horrid little pig found a huge pile of twigs. "These twigs will make a brilliant house for me!" he thought. But the little pig was even lazier than his brother . . .

. . . so the house was a disaster!
When the friendly wolf saw the
terrible tangle of twigs he thought,
"Goodness me! That house is an accident
waiting to happen. I'd better go and help!"

*Goodness
me!*

and I'll **puff**...

and I'll

THROW

YOU

RIGHT

OUT!"

"I'm sorry," sighed the wolf. "I only wanted to help."

How rude!

The third horrid little pig was SO lazy, he couldn't be bothered to build a house at all! So he found a nice, cosy chicken shed instead . . . and moved in.

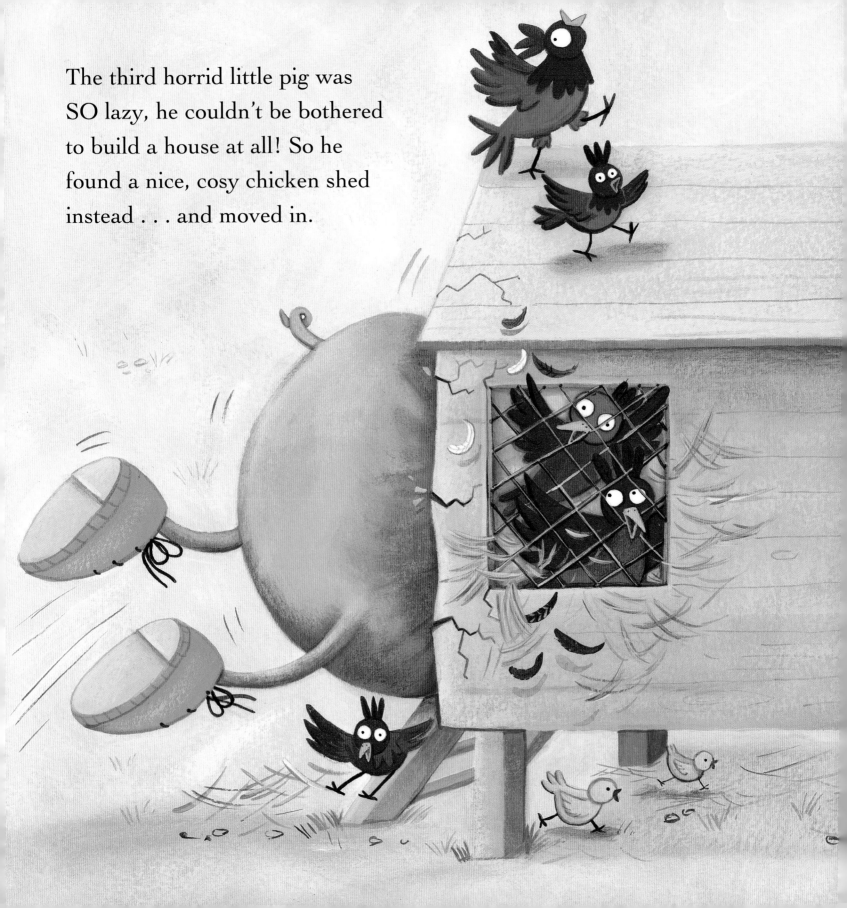

The friendly wolf just
happened to be passing.
"Oh my gosh!" he thought.
"Those poor chickens!
I must go and speak to that pig."

Pig's pinched our house!

HELP!

"Little pig, little pig, may I come in?"

"SHOVE OFF!" shouted the pig, rudely.

"Not by the hairs on my chinny chin chin will I let a WOLF in! Put one paw in my house and I'll **huff**...

and I'll

puff

and I'll . . ."

"Hold it right there!"
said the wolf. "This isn't YOUR
house. It's the chickens' house!"
"Who cares!" said the little pig.
"Now get lost, THE LOT OF YOU!"
What a horrid little pig he was.

Charming!

So the kindly wolf invited all
the chickens back to HIS house,
which was built from bricks
and was very strong indeed.

WOLF'S HOUSE

Meanwhile, the house built
by the first horrid little pig . . .

. . . was being eaten up
by a herd of hungry cows.

The house built by the
second horrid little pig . . .

. . . was being pulled apart
by a flock of angry birds.

And the third horrid little pig . . .

*You've nicked
our TWIGS!*

Our NESTS!

. . . was being
pecked by a
cockerel, and went **wee wee weeeeeeeeeee**, all the way back
eeeeeeeeeeee to his brothers
(which was *just* what
the cockerel wanted).

Now NONE of the pigs had a home. But the wolf did. And it looked very warm and cosy.

"This house would be perfect for us!" said the horrid little pigs.

So they waited until dark.
Then they climbed onto the roof
and began to slide down the chimney.
The wolf heard the horrid little pigs, so he got out a
GREAT, BIG POT OF BOILING ...

WOLF'S HOUSE

SOUP!

"You must be hungry!"
said the wolf.
He really was the
sweetest, loveliest wolf ever.

The friendly wolf let the pigs stay. And after a while they stopped being lazy, horrid little pigs and learned how to build a proper house made of bricks . . .

. . . which was big
enough for EVERYONE!

And they all lived
happily ever after.

The End